CHAPTER ONE

I'm telling this to you as I've simply run out of options. Maybe you aren't like the rest of them, perhaps you are, I'm not sure. Honestly, I don't know if it matters. So this is my life, and I need you to know that I'm currently happy and sad and wondering how this is.

I don't have any friends. I had a friend at work called Michael but one day he didn't show up. He always turned up, so I couldn't make sense of it, but then I heard he'd died. I suppose that cleared things up a little.

I think I broke down; it hurt that the

whole office knew before me, and it hurts that everyone is fighting over his old job, myself included. But I suppose that's these times for you. Each one of us is clambering up the rung of the ladder so we can reach a summit only plausible in our heads. Well, that's my theory on it anyway, but my wife has told me to stop thinking like this. So I have... or, well, at least I've tried.

Some of the women at work who were friendly with Michael have gone to some therapy sessions to contemplate any "issues" they may be having. I was concerned about going, especially when I turned out to be the only one there, apparently it's a woman's thing. This whole therapy malarkey is entirely new really, I think it will just be a phase, perhaps it's the smart thing to do, I don't know really.

You see in Michael's note he claimed that he was always too pressured in his job so maybe that was a reason for his actions. I don't want to speculate too much though

because I heard what he did caused a huge mess. Apparently the blood made the ink unreadable. Then again, I've heard there wasn't even a note. The truth is there probably isn't a truth to this story, and the best any of us can do is to move onwards and upwards.
Today I attended my last therapy session, but I'd never been back after the first time. When I went the 'specialist' asked me to say a few words about Michael. Apparently, it rationalized the grieving process. If I'm honest, I think they just want to make sure I'm not going to kill myself anytime soon. That way, they can ship me off and create space for a new client. But anyway, I said that I missed him and that he was nice, but that I don't understand why he did it. He was doing well in life, you see. He was a partner at the firm, had a wife, a mistress, owned shares in Ford, lived in the upper east side, and he was from a good heritage. He had it all going on.

The 'specialist' told me that all the material things in his life might still not have offered him happiness.

That's when I finally realized that the 'specialist' was an idiot and so I picked up my coat and left.

On the way home, I passed a car that reminded me of Michael; a Hudson Seven roadster, the same color blue he had with shined wheels and a smarmy driver to boot. That got me wondering where all his stuff was. He was buried over in Staton Island the other week. As funerals go, it was a strange one. His wife didn't seem to cry very much, considering the circumstances. This was easily explained though, as a few months ago, my wife heard from one of the pastor's lady friends that Michael's marriage was heading south.

Usually, I disregard gossip of this kind, but I think it may have held some truth to it as only last week I saw Michael's wife getting cozy with some flashy broker. If I'm frank this did surprise me as I always saw her as a sort of bug-eyed betty.

I accidentally took two wrong turns on the way home; I guess I had lots on my mind. I gave myself the benefit of the doubt though, you see, I've not been at my new place long, maybe a few months in total. When I finally got home, my wife was waiting for me.

"It's all wrong." she moaned. "All of it."

I uttered "what's wrong honey" in a weak attempt to sound energetic. "The decoration, it's just not right for the apartment it's...it's too traditional." Attempting to pacify her, I repeatedly praised the great job she had done decorating.
Realistically the decoration didn't retain an ounce of taste, but she can't fail expectations that I dare not make.

The living room was a sort of glazed bronze colour that just looked very much like a shiny brown. I think it was supposed to look regal. The wooden floors were draped over by a rug of a deep red

shade. Covering the windows were some thick curtains of the same color red and a large Chandelier inherited from my wife's mother hung over us.
"It's beautiful darling; all the other apartments around us look so
'pre-war' in comparison."
"Yes, but I don't want to compare the apartment to our current surroundings; I want to compare it to where we will be living."

This drove me back into my insecurity.

We had only just moved. I'd gotten her as close to the upper west side as my wage would allow, but it wasn't enough. She wanted to be closer to the fashionable areas, to acceptance.

"Well, for now, I think the place looks fine."

"Yes, I suppose it will do, we won't be here long though, we can move when you get your promotion can't we?" she asked, her eyes were full with the promise of a future. "Yes of course, if I get the partnership, we can move anywhere you want."

But then her face swelled with dreaded angst. "What do you mean if, I thought the decision was as good as made with what's his face out the picture."
I know she wasn't fully aware of the friendship I had with Michael, but that didn't stop it from stinging.

I scoured around my mind for a response, "Yes, erm well that has sort of opened up the field for me.""Good. I hope I don't come across callous by saying that his blunder may be the best thing that ever happened to your career, love."

As harsh as she was being, there was a truth to what she said.
Without Michael's death, a partnership position wouldn't have opened up for a long time. So morbidly, his curse could turn into my blessing.

The sentiment proves something my father told me right. Amongst the swarms of bullshit he threw my way in an attempt to keep me South he told me. "A man cannot rise without anymore without another falling; you may think you're on the rise now Jonny, but one day you'll plummet back to where you came from." Thinking about this depressed me a little, so I stopped or at least I tried to.

I always tried to ignore my father's tired pessimism. I'd just put it down to a resentment tied to his failures. My father had once been successful, but as he said: "that was in another lifetime." He made a great deal of money supplying uniforms for the war and then when that was all over, he poured all of his money into a ranch down south.

Right after the war, the farmers lost all of their subsidies and prices hit rock bottom. My father has been trying to sell his land ever since. To tell you the truth nobody's interested in some dried up land that dries up dreams. I always felt bad for my Pa, but he didn't help himself, he was a self-made man with a self-made idea of what life is like and this has left him closed off from the new opportunities opening up everywhere. When I told him of my plans to come to New York and make a man of myself, he roared with fierce dereliction. "You're making the same mistakes I did boy, I chased a dream to the edge of the earth, I caught it and took it for my own, and do you wanna know something, its empty, its false, and its broken. Do you want to end up like me? Learn your place and get used to it for the world has a way of dragging those who climb high back to their origins."

So you see that's why I don't like to think of him, he'd be jealous of me, he wouldn't understand.

Then a loud voice transcended from the hall, "So are we going out tonight?"

"Erm, yes honey."

"When?"

"Soon."

"Where?"

"I thought we could head to 21st." She wandered through to the dining room at this point "We've never been there, why should we go there?" Her voice carried faint skepticism.

"Well, I heard at work that its a very fashionable place to go, all the high flyers love it, from what I understand its a gathering spot for all those who have nothing better to do than gather," I said this as convincingly as I could, but not even the cold October air could make my mask stick.

In an attempt to sound only vaguely interested she nodded with agreement and spurted out "Well I suppose it couldn't hurt me to grace it with my presence, as long as I like the look of the people of course. After all, booze is booze, and a bar is a bar, but the quality of people can be so variable these days."

I was glad. The truth is I only wanted to go there because I was meeting a friend for advice and I didn't want my wife to know it was pre-planned. I find her attraction to the shininess of attention can shroud what's important sometimes.

"Shall I call my sister and tell her to meet us there?"

"Yes, call her up and plan to meet there at 10.30."

"That early, anyone who's anyone won't bother turning up before the clock strikes 11,00."

I was beginning to lose my line of patience. "Yes, well, some of us have work tomorrow, dear." I heard something along the lines of "What does that have to do with anything." But I'd I wandered into our bedroom by that point, leaving a trail of clothes in my wake, I had no clue what I should wear, but

I didn't need to, my wife had picked out a light gold shirt, tan slacks and a green jumper which had been laid out on the bed with careful consideration.

Our bedroom had been the last room to be redecorated. The walls had been covered with wallpaper of various platinum green shades, and when the lights shone in from advertisements outside the window, the room resembled Coney Island after dark. To me, it was all slightly overwhelming, but my wife likes them. In any case, it's an improvement on the cracked plaster and faded yellow walls that once resided the space and reminded me of my childhood home.

A calm wind entered the room from the balcony, and as I stepped out onto the cool tiles, I was taken aback by the evening air. It was fresh but still maintained the smell of the city. The fumes, the roaring sounds, the freedom, the money, it was all here, all accessible with one breath, and the more I inhaled, the more I wanted.

A new advertisement had been thrown up since I was last out there. It was for one of the more prominent, less reputable, stockbrokers. The sign claimed they could make "Any man from anywhere rich, in the fastest, easiest way possible." There was no information on how they would do this, but I suppose that isn't important. As long as the destination is clear, the journey should work itself out.

My money has been doing very well.
I invested a few summers ago now, and its value has increased by over eight-hundred percent. I frequently speak to my broker to see how it's doing. Every time I do his cool, rhythmic voice explains how my investments never stop going up. I have my Grandfather to thank really.

Some years ago now, my Grandfather left me a sum of money. I gave some to my father but kept the majority and for a long while, I left it alone. When I came to the city I was swept away by a wave of financial advancements that came after the war. Before I knew it some quiet advice from a stranger in a bar turned into a telephone call, and soon enough, I had shares for anything worth having shares in.

Sometimes I think I should release my investments and bank the money I have made, but every time I do I realize how much more I can make, besides I have been told by people who ought to know that my money would be more successful in stocks, so I've kept them in for now.

My wife called me, "are you done already?" I wandered back in and threw on my clothes in a disorderly fashion. She was waiting for me, leaning against the door wearing a green dress, almost emerald in shade. It wrapped tightly around her, and she wore it knowingly. To accompany her, she had white shoes that made her walk uncomfortably and a bag which she wore for the sake of wearing.

As I walked through to the hall, her expression ceased to be in its aimless, empty state and instead gained a serious composure. "What are you wearing? You look ridiculous, like a drunken clown." "Well, how can you claim that when you picked out my clothes?" The annoyance in my reply was masked by vague humor.

"I wouldn't have made my greatest enemy wear this monstrosity." "Well, perhaps I can just change into something quickly." Then she became severe "Just change that god-awful shirt, yellow is such a common-looking color." "Yellow? This is not yellow, its pale gold... it says so on the tag."

Her face was filled with reassurance "Gold, well if it claims its gold I suppose the outfit will do, I still think you could have a better taste though."

Occasionally, in moments such as that, I do wonder whether my wife contains so great a pride that admitting to imperfection would be blasphemous or so great an ignorance that remembering her actions is not considered necessary. I do love her, don't mistake that. But sometimes I can only see her imperfections, her outlandish presence and daggered gazes, her efforts for attention and her cries for pity. For brief moments this is all I can see. But luckily these moments are only fleeting, and then I go back to see the real her, the beautiful woman with a towering personality and quick wit, with humor and gratitude. And I realize, that is the women I married.

That evening when we were on our way to the bar, I'd had enough of her shit. When we got out of our apartment, it was too cold, so I offered her my jacket, a blue one from Paris. She told me she would rather freeze. Then when I called a cab over, she refused to get in as the smell was "unpleasant." So I had to wait another ten minutes to find a cab, in which time her pride still wouldn't allow her to wear something as unfashionable as a coat. So instead I had to

listen to insufferable whining.
When we eventually reached the bar, her disembodied frown transformed into excited smile as she saw the hordes of people trying to get in.
"Golly, I did not realize the exclusivity of the place, if I'd have known it was this lovely, I'd have dressed up."

I think that remark sounded less vain in her head.

We walked past what looked to be the owner of a bar talking to three cops, all of whom had corrupt eyes and pockets lined with cash. They were in dispute. I imagine it was over payment or something of the sort, but whatever it was it began to draw a crowd. The bar owner pulled out something with a metallic complexion that reflected loudly against the green and red lights of the street, it could have been a watch - I'm not sure. But anyway, he handed it to the cops, and after a momentary inspection, they nodded, and the issue appeared resolved. Around them he crowd was visibly disappointed at lack of a scene. When we walked through the first doorway, we encountered a few bootlegger boys. They looked my wife up and down and smirked, so I grabbed her arm tighter and knocked on the basement door.

The door was encased entirely in metal, it had no handle, and bolts on every corner. It was menacing. When the peephole opened with a loud scrape, I stepped back. This made the thugs snigger. With the peephole open we could faintly hear jazz music. A pair of weathered, yellow eyes came to look at us and asked us our name. The issue is with places like that they often don't let just anyone in, if they are quite full then they won't let some nobody in. My wife tried to answer, "he's called John Southla-"

"Michael Griswold," I interrupted.

The yellow eyes narrowed but after a sec-

ond or so the shutter abruptly closed, and the door opened.
The small yellow eyes belonged to a boy, about Sixteen and dressed similarly to the thugs.
We walked down some winding wooden stairs, stained with a decade of use, and then suddenly we were in a new world. New York cities very own
Eden.

The room was covered in a warm blue, with an Italian maple bar across one side and a full orchestra on the other. It was loud, and I could hear everything and nothing. The dance floor was full of color, people moved around with a grace only offered by a few drinks; entirely in time with the music offered by Paul Specht and his jazz band. Their audacity transcended the dancefloor and into the mood of the room, giving me the confidence of a man twice my value. It gave me a sense of enlightenment to be in a place with such a feeling, anything was possible here. Few other times could a business deal coincide to a proposal and both appear completely natural in their setting.

There were plenty of interesting characters in the club. A man no older than twenty had bought a table, and all the women on it in one corner. While an elderly lady was playing the gamblers at their own game in the other. It was a spectacle only conceivable in New York.

I stood next to a young girl at the bar. She wore a silver dress beneath her dark curls and pale

skin and was batting off the attention of a man many rings below her worth. He was a coarse, fat fellow with an uneducated accent. His florid attempts to gain her favor went ignored, and eventually, his intoxication led him to kneel down and form some sort of proposal. She waited until she had received her drinks then stepped over him and claimed he'd "had his chance." A tall man of culture then appeared and took her to the happiness of the dance floor, where she hoped to stay fixed in time.

I was so transfixed in the film scene around me that I didn't even register my wife's company.

Then my wife interjected, “Why did you say your name is...?"
"It just made getting in easier." I replied in a way that should warrant no further questions. Naturally, she didn't take the hint.
"Yes, but why does a different name make things easier?"
"People who go to places like this have reputations carried by names, Michael has one of those names, we don't."
She seemed agitated by this comment like it was something she didn't already know. Then suddenly she disappeared into the sea of color, probably to forget her reality.

I wandered around the bar until I found my colleague. He was sitting at the back

watching events unfold from the security of the shade. He's called Mark Devlin, and he's the first person I met in this town. Initially, I saw him as a man of honor, but a realist would see him as a man of resourcefulness. Being a working man in his forties he wore a deep brown suit and a tie loosely around his neck, he had a cigar in one hand and a drink in the other.
"About time you showed up young Chap, what kept you? Was it that piece of work you're still holding onto?"

With his infectious smile, the comment was somehow not rude. "Oh, it was something like that, what's not keeping a guy busy anymore?" I replied. I asked him how his travels went, and he talked of his journey to all the European capitals.
"I mean I loved Rome and Paris and Monte Carlo, they are so full of art and culture. The quaint streets make one feel far more significant than the gaping avenues of Manhattan." He was trying to explain the subtle differences between Europe and

America. He's British, you see.

He then told me, "so you see it was interesting to walk through the ancient cities, interesting to see the origins of our culture. Take London, you know I was born there,don't you, old Chap?"

I nodded.

"Well when I grew up there, we always saw America as its own land separate from us entirely, but I believe its a land created from the..."
"Oh my god, Jonny, you're here!" I didn't even have to turn around to realize it was my sister in law,
Carolina. I looked behind me to find a woman a few years younger than my wife, she had long dark hair held in place by a red ribbon, smooth, fair skin, and deep blue eyes which darted between myself and Mark. She wore a crimson dress, almost covered entirely by a perfectly white blouse.

I asked her if my wife was having fun, and I received a shrug. She sat and greeted both of us. "So how's life treating you, Carolina?"

"Ah, you know very busy, I've nearly school and have some essays to hand in before the end of the month, but it'll all be over soon."

Carolina is in Law School at Barnard College. She rings me up for advice sometimes but I don't really know much about it. My wife disapproves of it privately. As once she told me Carolina was out of her depth and needed to learn her place.

Mark seemed interested in what
Carolina was saying and moved his head out of the shadow.

He asked her if she wanted to be a lawyer and when she replied yes, an almost hidden smirk appeared on his lips. Carolina clearly became uncomfortable but kept eye contact with him, holding it until he

turned away. In her mind, she thought she had won, but in his head, he believed she was deluded.
Then my wife came over.

She spoke in a very loud tone. "My goodness it's hot in here, don't you think it's hot in here? I'm so hot honestly, I could drink gallons of water."

She'd drunk gallons of something, but it wasn't water. As words spilled out of her, the liquor poured in.

"Jonny, I love you. Why don't we come here more often, I'm so glad I decided to go out tonight, Jonny wanted to stay in the little urchin."

She was pretty volatile and made even less sense than usual, but eventually, her transparent drunkenness became annoying to us; so we just ignored her.

My conversation with Mark eventually transported itself from light, small talk to the matter at hand by the time a few

rounds had passed by, and things got very interesting very quickly.
"So what is the situation with your work-place at the moment, old Chap?" "A position has opened up for a partnership in the firm, and I threw my name in for consideration, but I know there is competition so
I'm just uneasy about the whole situation. I have lots riding on this promotion, you know."

"Well, as you know, I have lots of connections within and around your firm, and it's known that these positions do rarely arise." I nodded apathetically, god I do know these things. Honestly, I don't know what it is with the British and arrogance sometimes. "And obviously it is going to be very difficult for you to obtain considering others' advantages." I again nodded apathetically, Jesus Christ he treats me like I don't work there already.

"But I do know a way in which you can

secure the job, it's done all the time." He took a red pen and some paper from his pocket and scribbled something on it. He then told me to take it, consider the offer and get in touch if I'm interested. He folded the note and slipped it across the table, standing up to put on his blazer. He told me goodnight and walked away through the crowds of drunken dancers, his suit becoming redder in the light.

CHAPTER TWO

The city had a cold edge that morning and the paths in Central Park were beginning to be covered in brown shades of autumn. I was walking briskly amongst crowds of the similarly minded towards my work, and I felt a sense of optimism. I left my wife in bed, she most likely won't awake until noon. After yesterday I was a little more at ease with my job situation. I needed to call up Mark to ask some questions about the proposal, but if I can just sort things out with my broker, it can't be an issue.

I walked down William Street towards the office. I felt uneasy. I knew following through with Mark's plan was wrong, paying for things that shouldn't be bought is always wrong, yet the offer is just too tempting to turn down. I always planned on making it on my own through my own abilities.

When I was younger, I held on to the belief that my potential could get me where I wanted to go, but over the past few years, I have become a realist. A realist would say that you either need luck or money to succeed. I'd probably run out of luck soon as that kind of luxury doesn't stick around for in my family too long. But money, well I have some of that. This reassured me as luck and money are basically the same things these days. So really there is no need for me to feel guilty about the whole situation as I am merely doing what others would do if they had my ingenuity. I walked into a store and bought a newspaper to take my mind of the whole situation. I still couldn't shake the guilt though.

I bought The New Yorker and The Wall Street Journal, although another paper caught my eye. It was from some small, more irrelevant publisher I haven't heard of, but the title caught my eye, so I took a copy and read it on the bench.

Wake up New York

Condemn me if you must, yet I saw economic policy and propaganda being made in close relief. My conclusion? The low opinion I held of government before I went to Washington was not elevated by participation in it. I saw a complete disconnect between reality—the economics and proper politics. We are under false pretenses, the
Federal Reserve has scaled down our economy to dust. The only issue is we do not know it.

The more cynical of us here today will be nonplused by my observation. On the other hand, the more earnest of us realizes that the continuing disconnect

between intervention and our scientific knowledge of recessions is a disaster because "The main issues of present-day politics are essentially economic," according to leading politicians.

If I put this latest recession in context. It was over eight years ago, and it was brief, so we have forgotten the signs, the signs being shown when the administration took office when a downturn was already underway. The president and his coterie blamed their predecessors like they blame WW1 and Europe for the social disconnect in this country.

Politics and mainstream economists believe our "capitalist" economy depends on sustaining "confidence."
This month the president's chief economic adviser wrote in The Wall Street Journal. "Because confidence is so important for spending decisions, the decreasing number of jobs since September created the risk of a self-fulfill-

ing prophecy of low demand and weaker employment. That's why the recent upturn in employment is particularly good news." Wall Street or Washington, D.C., these economists are all Keynesians now — they believe that boosting spending and keeping it pumped up are the keys to prosperity. They know a lot that just ain't so, but they know enough is amiss in our
R18631X0457
R24126N0457
R20470L0457
"fundamentally sound economy" to have only named a "Strong crisis manager". As president of the New York Federal Reserve Bank claims.

The last so-called free-market recession was scary, if not brief. The Harding administration followed standard federal tradition and stood by and allowed it to happen because "everything was overly high" after the world war and recession was something that
"ran its course, like measles". There was

political pressure to intervene, but the favored theory of earlier business crises carried the day one last time: "Businessmen got themselves into this mess, so let them get themselves out of it."

We know how counterproductive these interventions could have been anyway. Whenever government intervenes in the market, it aggravates rather than settles the problems it has set out to solve. This is a general economic law of government intervention. We need to use every modern economic 'tool,' every device of progressive and 'enlightened' economics, every facet of government planning, to combat an economic downturn. For
the first time, we should throw laissez-faire overboard and throw every government weapon into fixing inflated stocks and saving what's left beneath our economy's facade.

What they know in Washington is "smart

politics". Policies consist of happy talk, reassurance that all is well, that it's all under government control, and extravagant use of the propaganda and bold statements. All governments are firmly committed to the policy of low-interest rates, credit expansion, and inflation. When the unavoidable aftermath of these short-term policies appears, they know only of one remedy-to pursue inflationary ventures. But explaining this tragic situation goes beyond the direct policy-makers. Two further groups not inside Washington, D.C., deserve mention too: economists and the public.

First, economists have superficially treated monetary problems, failing to integrate money into their theory of markets.
They naively embraced the neutral approach of money, failing to appreciate how financial manipulation necessarily distorts markets and causes booms followed by corrective busts.

Hence, Benjamin Strong, governor of the New York Federal Reserve Bank, has kept silent and allowed the public to be misleading. In my opinion, no misunderstanding in economic science has done more harm than the role of money and credit in business boom and bust.

Second, the myopic public disposition for lower interest rates by allegedly costless credit expansion creates an irresistible temptation for politicians, bureaucrats, and economists to comply. But I suppose the theory of democracy surely applies all too well here: the public gets what it wants, good and hard.

To be honest, I didn't understand most of the stuck up terminology, I'm a lawyer and not an economist after all. I did know that the article is the biggest pile of crap I have ever read, which is embarrassing as I have seen many of my wife's 'Homemaking Journals'.
Really the article was probably from one

of those liberal-minded fools who publicize their beliefs and draw in do-gooders. Personally, I don't believe in handouts, you should have to earn what you get in life.

I switched over to reading The Wall Street Journal. Their articles thoroughly discredited the trash I'd just digested. I'm pretty sure slander like that shouldn't be publicized because I guarantee you, people with less sense than myself would fall for it and they'd be sent into a panic. I placed the New Yorker and Wall Street Journal under my arm, dusted myself off and walked to work. In a considerably worse mood than when I had set out.

I got into work for 8:20, which is a little early, so the reception was emptier than usual. It's a lovely modern building. All the interior walls are painted stark white with large windows covering the front walls. There is a wooden staircase spiralling through the middle of the room and desks dotted across the cramped floor space.

Light spilled across the floor as the sun rose to illuminate the room, it turned the white walls yellow and added a sense of warmth. The heating was still broken though, so the light did nothing to heat the reception. My workplace has been cold for a long time, they claim it's going to be fixed soon, but nothing seems to be getting done. It's crazy really, for all the money spent on modern architecture and materials we still freeze in the winter, but I guess as my wife claims... beauty is pain, and pain is worth it.

The only other people in at this time were the receptionists and secretaries sat behind their desks, each of them has a familiar faces. But I couldn't name them. I walked by them and received a nod from a smartly dressed, if not plain-looking woman who had distant grey eyes beneath thick-rimmed spectacles. She looked empty inside, but I suppose obeying commands from a telephone all day does that to people.

As my feet climbed the hard wooden steps, I found the rest of the building to not be so quiet. The office was not empty; it was chaotic. The faint yellow walls were covered with paper, the floor was being trampled by an army of busy workers. More desks had been moved into the already cramped room, and in the corner, three people were arguing stressfully over a broken typewriter. I had a free typewriter over by my area, but I kept that quiet as I might have needed it at some point. I darted over to my desk to find two men looking over some contracts. One of them was wearing a very light grey suit with a gold tie, his mousy brown hair was being combed back with that new Brylcreem stuff, and he seemed very serious like he was posing or something, guys like him try a little hard if I'm honest. The other, taller guy was standing up looking over him, he was reading the pages but appeared tired, or hungover. I'm guessing tired as he on his two second cup of coffee. His eyes sprinted across the pages, but he said nothing, the man sat down was definitely in charge.

They looked up at me, acknowledged my presence, then returned to the urgency of their work. "Excuse me,"I muttered to the two men. I didn't think they heard me. "So... what's going on, why's everything so crazy?" This time I'd added a little volume.

They had to have heard me, but still no response. They didn't even have the decency to pretend to notice me. The two men dared to work with their crap at my desk and ignore me. I bet they're drug store cowboys in their spare time, wouldn't surprise me.
I decided to go and find out what was happening, I have never seen pandemonium like this in all my time at the firm. I

walked over to the far side of the room by the partner's offices, which all have glass windows looking into them.
They were all covered by blinds, well almost all of them - one office remained empty with the light switched firmly off.
As I was about to knock on the door, it swung open and one of the senior partners – Elliot Dangerfield faced up to me.
"John, what are you doing here? You're supposed to be on the case, it been brought forward again, we have a little over two days."

I tried desperately to hide my surprise and confusion. I mean the case I assumed he was talking about wasn't due for three weeks. I wasn't even in charge. I'm not yet a partner after all.

Elliot clearly hadn't noticed the hidden shock written over my face as he went on to discuss how the old partner, Jay Atkins, had been transferred to the flagship case, so I alongside someone else was taking complete control over the laundering case.

I held slight satisfaction that I was picked to take over. But I also had a faint heart attack as we needed a case built in two days.

I asked Elliot why the office had transcended into a state of pure madness. He informed me that the flagship case had also been brought forward and was scheduled just after mine. Then I informed him of my desk situation, and he told me to take the empty office. I walked back through the office to my desk, the two men had been joined by a shorter, broad man who I spoke to once at lunch on my first day. The eye contact I made with him was a little awkward as he never talked to me again and obviously didn't want to. I maneuvered myself around the three men and grabbed some case files. For some reason, half of them were missing, I was sure I had left them on my desk, but clearly they had been lost in the mountains of paper now covering my workspace. I also looked for my typewriter, that was something less easily hidden. The men became increasingly agitated as I scarpered around. One said, "What are you doing? I'm trying to work here." He sounded annoyed as he said it, borderline angry.

"Well... erm, I'm just looking for my typewriter, have you seen it anywhere? It was on my desk just last night."

The stubby guy told me the typewriter was not here when he arrived but that he heard some people were looking for one. He couldn't look me in the eyes when he said it though.

I searched around the office for a short while, but eventually I just gave up and went to Michael's old office. The light was now on, but when I reached the door, I hesitated to push it open. I stood

outside the door for no less than five minutes, contemplating.
Is it right that I stand where my friend once stood? Is it acceptable for me to take his job? Should I dare to climb as high as him, a man born into success?

These questions were eventually answered for me as soon enough the door opened. On the other side was a woman stood holding my missing files, she stared at me as if she knew me, as if she sort of understood. But that's probably me being melodramatic, it’s a bad habit I've picked up from my wife.

She was average in height with a slim build and her hair cut short. Beneath the files, I could see she wore a white shirt that was buttoned all the way up and tucked into a seamlessly black skirt. She was dressed ready for the job and judging by the look of her tired eyes she had been doing her work through the night. Which is impressively dedicated for an assistant.

Just as I walked in, she dumped the files into my arms and sarcastically informed me "It's about time you showed up." I took it as a joke on the surface, but I'm don't think assistants are supposed to speak to the lawyers in such a way. Anyway, I smiled at her as I placed the books down, I then asked her if she could grab me a coffee. I even told her she should get herself one. Instead of following instructions, she just sat down and went through the files, I left her to it, but I will say the impressive dedication I thought she had was clearly a misjudgement.

The room did not retain a hint of Michael. All of his things had been moved out, the bright colors he once decorated the room with had been replaced by freshly painted, grey walls, a cleaned carpet, and an empty desk. His memory had been wiped from every square inch of the place. All of this depressed me a little, so I tried to distract myself with work. I couldn't concentrate though, the firm, its reaction to his death and its eulogy the senior partner read began the circle around my head.

"Mrs. Griswold, family members, colleagues, and friends. Sorrow fills our hearts this sad moment, a sadness that is deep and personal. Michael has silently closed the door of life and departed from us. Our lives will be empty in the areas that he had brightened for us.
Albert Einstein says, "The value of a man should be seen in what he gives and not in what he can receive." In one word, Michael was a man who gave. He gave much to his work, to his family, to everyone. That is why ladies and gentlemen as we are gathered here to say goodbye to him, I would like to speak in celebration of his life. Here was an existence that demanded notice, a life that exemplified brilliance, an experience that inspired emulation, a life that burned so that others' paths were lit. Michael first came to our firm when he was just an un-

trained young man, he gradually became a strategic thinker, a visionary who was brilliant, innovative, and creative. As such, he contributed much to the development of the....."

The whole speech the senior partner gave was a lie. The firm didn't care he was gone, they only care about looking like they care, it's all an act really. I became increasingly frustrated until the door flew open, and Elliot barged in. "Ah, great, you've met, I don't believe you've worked with John yet, have you, Rosalie?" Then suddenly, the morbid considerations left my mind, replaced by reality. "No, I haven't had the pleasure before now." She then told Elliot all about her excitement to work with me. Most of what she said bypassed my ears.

I will say from what I saw Elliot was acting oddly, he seemed very interested in Rosalie, it's possible they know each other from outside work or something.

Honestly, I wouldn't know. Elliot then told Rosalie. "You'll do a great job, better than any of those knuckleheads out there, there's a reason we picked you for the job." By this point, Elliot's hand had moved from the table to Rosalie's lap, I pretended to be engrossed in my work and pulled my eyes away. The next thing I knew he was walking out, turning around at the door telling us "oh, by the way, we are pretty understaffed currently so we can't give you and assistants or secretaries for the case, so you'll have to manage."

A wave of realization then washed over me, Rosalie wasn't a secretary, but she was also a lawyer alongside me.

If I'm honest, I was a little surprised. I mean, I'd heard of these so-called modern women rising through the working world, but I hadn't actually witnessed it. A part of me wondered about Rosalie's ability, she may have earned her position, or she may have earned Elliot's affection, either way, I had to work with her as my equal.

After an hour of silent work, Rosalie gave me back my missing files. They had ink covering them. She'd worked through every inch of information.

"There wasn't much we didn't already know, but some of the sections I've underlined definitely reinforce our standpoint on the case. One recurring detail I've noticed is the lack of substantiated evidence from a party without a motive to pin everything on Chauncey. We can easily argue he is being set up to cover up a larger scheme of fraudulent behavior..." "Yes, but what evidence do what have to support the idea that there is a larger scheme at work?"I questioned.

My reply was sharply direct, but if I'm honest she didn't appear to be thinking like a lawyer, but instead, she sounded like a girl whose ideas appear far brighter in her head.

Then she surprised me.

"Well if you look at the company's file you can see the amount of unaccounted revenue from overestimated stocks far outweighs the value of which Chauncey is charged for, the company's motive lies within the fact they'd rather protect their fraudulent stock scheme over Chauncey's freedom. Chauncey is basically a pawn for their well -oiled embezzlement scheme, he's far more expendable than he realized which is why it was so easy for the company to isolate their illegality to him. "Hesitation filled her face. "Well, this is what we can argue anyway."
I didn't bother withholding my smile well. I'm not sure Rosalie understood that she had found the basis of our case.

CHAPTER THREE

I worked in the office through the night. I had given my wife a call telling her I wouldn't be home. Naturally, she wasn't impressed, but it wasn't the first time I've worked all night, and it most likely won't be the last. As my professor at Columbia told me once. If there is a temptation, there will be a crime. So far, this sentiment has turned out to be accurate. I have always been in work because New York is a city built on the temptations of the ambitious.

The office had reached a state of idle busyness, everyone was still working, but tiredness had become a natural state for most. Plants in the corner were slowly dying, as the day progressed the heat built up, and the plants been watered in days. The heat of the place was drying them up. I would have watered them myself but I was too busy. The case I was on held more importance than some stupid plants. In the corner of the office, I spotted a young guy, no older than twenty-three, sleeping. He had fallen asleep into his books and most likely would be awoken to the panic of being behind his deadlines. In fairness, I can imagine how hard he must have been worked. When I received my first case here, after just joining the firm, I was required to go three nights without sleep. All the associates and partners dumped their analysis work on me. It was mind-numbingly dull, and in the morning, when they all came in to find their work completed on their desk, they quickly checked through it to see if anything useful had arisen.

For the most part, everything was disregarded, but if they did find some helpful information, I can't remember. I would have been too tired to care anyway.

Next to the young guy sleeping, there were two men arguing. I can't tell over what. I wandered over to see, but I tripped over a bin. Some fool had left it right in the middle of the floor. The bin crashed into the desk opposite me, and revealed a typewriter that was hidden behind it. I recognized it. It was bronze-colored with a white stripe moving across it. In its top corner, the initials B.M.R were engraved. They were the initials of the man I bought it from when I was at college. Someone had clearly broken my typewriter and forgot to tell me, or just didn't care enough to. I have an idea of who it was, most likely those losers who were at my desk the day before. Honestly, I was pretty annoyed about it, I still am actually. It's the type of dishonesty I never had to deal with growing up, but that's probably just the Christian in my upbringing.

I disconnected the telephone usually placed on my desk and carried it into Michael's office, just in case Mark rang. Rosalie hadn't left the office either. We made a pretty good team, if I'm honest. Her competence was pretty impressive. Rosalie was on the telephone to Chauncey and appeared to be having trouble getting through to him. I was trying to listen in, but there was a constant buzz of work in the background interrupting my hearing
After about half an hour, with
Rosalie still being talked down to,
I was about to wander over and try to resolve the issue. Right when I stood up the ringing of my telephone pulled me back to my chair. I dreaded another rant from my wife. It wasn't my wife though, it was someone who's of far more use to me.

A charismatic voice echoed through the line,

"Hello old chap, how're things?" It took me a moment to consider who I was talking to.
"Well Mark it's hectic to be honest, I'm sorry I haven't been able to get back to..."
"Oh don't talk nonsense John, I do nothing but sit here in my office all day. I have people to do my real work for me." I think he was trying to be comical, but I can't say for sure, I'm awful at this telephone thing.
"Sorry old chap but I don't have much time, so just checking in to see if you've gotten everything in place for my proposal."
I explained that I had been swamped with work, but I would get to it straight away.
"Well alright then, I don't know how much longer my offer can stay open..."
"No don't worry I'll sort it out now and give you a call back as soon as possible, I really am serious I'm sorry if-" I was then cut off.
"Oh, don't worry old chap I can wait until this evening. But I don't enjoy being

messed around." The telephone then rang dead, and a wave of panic circled around me.

I rushed back to my desk, its intruders had fallen asleep by this point, so I slid their crap out the way and picked up my contact book.
Racing back to the office, I dialled my broker's number and it began ringing.
Eventually, a very smooth voice full of assured confidence answered the telephone.
"Hello, its Marshall, who is this?"
"It's John... John Southland" The telephone line echoed silence.
"You know from the firm down by..." "Oh lawyer John, how are you doing?
You must know that your stocks are doing so well, one of the best. Krueger himself has complimented your selection."

I wanted the conversation to be brisk. I was busy you see, and Marshall is very smooth. If I got drawn into the conversation, I would have lost focus on my object-

ive.
"Yes, I'm glad. So I'm calling to ask if I can liquidate my stocks into cash as I'm in a tight spot at the moment and I could use the money."

I could hear Marshall thinking through the telephone.

"How many of your stocks exactly?" He asked, warily. "All of them." I replied. Silence then continued to fill the conversation until finally, he answered me.
"Well, you see John... it's just I have an inclination the stocks are going to shoot up within the week, they're on an incline since the small dip a month ago." His voice spoke to me as fluid as ever.
"What dip a month ago?" I inquired. "Regardless." He replied. "I don't think extracting your investments now is sensible. Say... wait a few days; they'll go up considerably and you'll be kicking yourself if you take your money now." I replied warily and told him I needed the money soon.

"Nonsense." I was told. "You can wait until say... Tuesday. Yes, Tuesday. By then, the stocks will have reached their potential. Don't you agree?" His silky voice led me to the answer he wanted to hear, and I still don't know why I let it happen.
"Yes," I replied apprehensively. "I guess I can hold out until Tuesday."
Marshall then attempted to create small talk but I could see right through it. I certainly trust him, but sometimes his falsities are transparent. I wasn't really pleased if I'm honest. I really just wanted the security of my money, but I had a gut feeling Marshall is right. If I'd have been rash and taken all my money out I would be kicking myself down the line.

After I closed the line with Marshall, I called up Mark to tell him the situation and he didn't seem impressed. But I explained to him the situation and that my interview for the job was on Friday meaning the decisions should be released no time before Tuesday anyway, so they'll get their money either way. To be honest, Mark was just kicking up a fuss for his own self-interest. He definitely just wanted to get his cut as soon as possible so he can move on to another venture; I preferred to protect my own interests... it's the only way to act nowadays.

After putting the telephone down on Mark the tether to my desk was broken, Rosalie was still having trouble with Chauncey. It was becoming increasingly heated. I went over and swiftly took over the call from her. I gave her a reassuring smile. She seemed somewhat relieved.

"Hello Courtney, what's going on?" I asked. "Oh not much John, it's just your colleague Rose stinks of incompetence. You should see some sense and fire her. Whoever thought it was a good idea to let women have proper jobs is such a-"
"Well, what was the issue that needs resolving?" I cut in. "Oh just something to do with a new plan, she hardly ex-

plained it properly so I don't understand it." He replied. I signalled Rosalie to pass me the sheet she made detailing our new plan of action. I recited it word for word quite slowly. When I was done, Chauncey seemed satisfied claiming, "You actually understand what I'm talking about Jonny boy." He really pissed me off if I'm honest. The rest of the day was much of the same, Rosalie and I worked late, I left the office around nine and she told me she wouldn't stay too much longer, I knew it was a lie. I told her she should get some sleep before the big day, she clearly had other plans though.

I strolled home under the black sky. The city was relatively quiet. It was the time of day when the workers stopped working and the partygoers were yet to party. For a brief moment New York seemed to lack purpose. As I walked through the park, colorful worries filled my head, and grey realities seemed ever closer. I knew I'd prepared for the case as well as I could, but my mind still ran with panic whenever I thought of it. The fate of my promotion now rested on factors out of my control, I'd done everything in my power to ensure success. Still though, I worried. I worried about these things only when I had nothing better to do. It's pathetic really.

I must have been in a daze of thought because I didn't even realize the cab's presence. I was knocked to the ground somewhere between the sidewalk and the park. Being so caught up in thought that you walk into a cab is an embarrassing event. The driver got out and hurled some casual abuse in my direction. I dusted myself off quickly, I felt as if the eyes of New York were laughing at me.
Walking significantly faster than before I eventually got home. The entire place was stifling hot. I could hear my wife in the bathroom, but I daren't interrupt her when she's getting ready. After throwing the windows open, I walked across our bedroom. I just wanted a bath really but

that would have to wait. I changed into nightwear then fell into my bed without thinking. Moments into my sleep my wife woke me up with a sense of urgency.

"Oh, I didn't hear you come in? How long have you been back? Goodness, I haven't seen you for so long!"
She asked me all of these questions in quick succession. "Yes, well you were in the bathroom when I got back so I didn't disturb you." She folded my clothes away and sat beside me on the bed, leaning into my chest. I just laid there for a short while, enjoying the silence. Eventually, I had to get up and bath. My wife had already eaten, but she made me some dinner while I was bathing. She came in with some fresh clothes and sat beside me. We talked about our days, mine was busy where hers was bland so we were both pretty somber.

"I would ask if you wanted to come out, but I can see you're tired. I'm just meeting some of the girls from school days. All we talk about is our husbands and our dresses, I'm not sure you'd find it interesting."

She was right, I can barely listen to their drivel at the best of times, so I'm glad my sanity was spared. "Oh yes, I'm certain you'd have a far better time without me," I replied. "Not to mention I have court tomorrow so I can't be tired. Do you need me to take you down or pick you up tonight?"

"Oh, don't worry about that dear, I'll take a cab there and back. You just rest well." With that, she got up and went to finish getting ready. After another short while I dried off and changed, walking into the kitchen to find her fully dressed up and ready to go. She was looking tall with some pearl-colored high heeled shoes on. She wore a sheer pink skirt with a white buttoned-up blouse. There wasn't much makeup covering her face - the way I like it. "You look beautiful," I told her. Honestly, she did, she looked younger, with a freshness to her complexion that I'd rarely seen since we married. She smiled graciously and told me she'd have looked better if I gave her some money for new clothes. I told her I would sort some out for her. The next moment she was out the door, and I was left with a chicken dinner and a night to fill with sleep.

CHAPTER FOUR

I've never been good at waking up early, my brother says it runs in the family. When I was younger, my old man sent me to live in England with my Aunt for a few years, I still don't know why. Anyway, the school I attended was a boarding school and I would never go a week without being punished for my sleepiness. It got very bad at one point. I was being shaken awake by what I thought was my friend Albert, I rolled over to find out it wasn't Albert I had called a hinkty but my headmaster. Needless to say, I was hanged, drawn and quartered, my ass became a target for cane practise and I had to stand for a week. It was another type of embarrassing.

The morning of court was no different, I got out of bed at just gone five, my eyes were hitting the floor, and though I was conscious, it would take a while for me to be present in the world. I headed out to the balcony for some fresh air. The city was a silent, unmoving beast at this time. The only people I spotted were some workers up high making some repairs on the billboards opposite me. I guess they had to be finished before everyone woke up. I didn't have much time, so getting changed and cleaned up went by in a haze. Looking for my wallet held me up, I wanted to leave my wife some money for the new clothes she wanted. I eventually spotted it on the floor by the dresser. When I bent down, I noticed our platinum green wallpaper was peeling at the edges, revealing ragged, cracked grey plaster from before the war. I'd have to tell my wife later, she wouldn't have been too happy if I woke her then.

If there's one thing I can rely on to wake me up it's New York's icy winter air. Even layers on layers of warm clothing couldn't protect me from the cold, I guess it made me walk that little bit faster. The view from my balcony didn't lie to me when it revealed an empty city. Some of the lights may have still been burning bright, but the people were in hibernation, I only saw one thing of interest on my walk. There was a group of twenty-somethings stumbling out of a bar just off fifth and Park. An odd mixture with far more money than taste. Two of the men wore bright yellow jackets covering white shirts that clearly looked better at the start of their evening adventure. Their trousers were a shiny black, and they wore an odd set of shoes, but their overload of alcohol clearly didn't permit them to care. One of the ladies wore a subtle blue dress that she would probably only be seen in once. Unlike her companions, she had the correct shoes, but she had been taken them off so she could walk. The other woman was noticeably younger. She wore a red dress with a rip down the side and made a half-hearted attempt to cover her modesty. Wearing one of the men's ties around her neck like a collar, she complained she couldn't find her purse, clearly unaware it rested on her shoulder. They all pilled into the Rolls Royce that pulled up beside them and shot off into the morning sunrise, leaving a shoe, wallet and some dignity on the sidewalk.

That class of youngsters isn't uncommon in New York. They are of the generation that finds work unfashionable and so replaces it with partying as their sole occupation. Their parents often act as clients for me; they are the easiest group to defend. Most have established familial roots in New York's' social scene which affords them connections across the legal and political realms of the city, meaning my work is merely a formality, but my fees are

nonetheless handsome. I suppose some could claim I'm of the lost generation, but I haven't really had the privilege of not being able to care about my future. I had a comfortable upbringing with my
British education and once wealthy father, but I alienated my advantages when I defied my pre-planned destiny and moved to New York for college. It was a risk that will soon pay off. I haven't visited my father in seven years, but I will definitely make contact from the Upper West Side apartment I'll be sure to buy when I make partner.

The cold weather made the walk to work feel eternal. Eventually I got to the front desk and made my way up to my office. The floor space was less filled than the day before but the most committed workers were still sat at their desks: some sleeping, some just waking up and the rest trying to work themselves to a raise.

I walked into a surprise when I opened

the office door. Elliot Dangerfield pushed passed me with haste. When I walked in, I found Rosalie sat amongst a lake of paperwork, crying into her sleeve. I shut the door and stepped across, bending over to see what was wrong. “Rosalie, what’s going on? Have you been kicked off the case or something?” I racked my brain, trying to find the source of her upset. Telling me “it doesn’t matter”, Rosalie walked out of the office, returning moments later with an empty box. She began with her desk, pilling all her belongings into a box with no real objective other than to leave as quickly as possible.

I kept on questioning her. It seemed no use. The confident woman of the day before had been replaced by a shell who wasn’t able to translate her anguish into words.
After only a few minutes, her box was filled, and she put on her pearl coat.

“Jonny, please... please could you give Elliot this." She had given me a short letter of resignation, it contained ink blots brought on by tears and little in the form of a reason for her departure. Just as she was about the open the door, I put my foot on the door, blocking her way. She glared at me, her cracked voice telling me to move out the way. I refused, telling her to sit down. After an exchange of glares, she complied and moved across to the desk. "Rosalie, what is going on? Yesterday you were all over this case, excited to prove yourself and suddenly I come in and you've cried all over the place, packed your things and want to resign without a clear reason. "I spoke softly, but if I'm honest the last thing I needed right then was silly drama, I didn't think Rosalie was the type, but I guess Women aren't used to workplace pressures.

Eventually, she plucked the courage to speak. "I thought I could do it, all of this, but I've been kidding myself all these years." She'd stopped crying but her voice still cracked every few words. "What has happened though, yesterday you were confident we could win this." When I was replying, I noticed Elliot peering through the door. I locked eyes with him, he looked uneasily as he turned from my sight. "Is it Elliot?" I questioned, "did he say something to you?" The redness on her face was replaced by white shock. "What did he say to you?" I asked. "What did he say?" I repeated. "Rosalie, what did he -"

"He tried to... I stopped him but... but, he wouldn't get off-" she sobbed.

I was surprised, but the more I think about it now, the less shocked I am. It's the kind of thing a guy like Elliot would try. He's probably one half of a stale marriage, looking for a chance to use his senior position to get lucky. Dirty little creep.

"When you say he touched you, do you mean -"
"Yes, he told me he had the power to make

or break me, and that I owe my success to him because -. " Crying interrupted her speech, so I pulled her into a hug.

In the end, she calmed down enough to give me the full story. Elliot had been making her uncomfortable for a little while, you know, getting a little close a little often, asking distasteful questions. That type of thing. When she came in early this morning, he took his shot. After Rosalie refused, he became vulgar, acting rather aggressively. This was just before I arrived. No wonder he scurried out so quickly.

"Rosalie, what do you want to do?". Her face moved into thought and uttered a single word. "Nothing." "What, no!" I pleaded. "Rosalie you've got to do something. I'm sure what he tried to do is - "

"Don't be so stupid Jonny, the best thing we can do is nothing."

"But why? What are you so afraid of?" I questioned.

"Jonny this isn't how the world works, this isn't some fairy-tale in which the villain is brought down, and the victim is heralded. This is real life. Elliot's Great Grandpa is one of the founders of this firm, his father is one of the most powerful, fierce judges in New York. We are just some nothings trying to become something."

Her words hit me hard, not because they were cruel but because they were true, they were a sad truth.
I had to run to the bathroom quickly. I can't have been more than five minutes, but when I got back, Rosalie's desk was bare, she had taken everything worth taking. There was a note on the table left for me. "Dear Jonny, I'm sorry. You can do this."

And so I did, or at least I planned to. I picked up her salmon shaded files and bolted out the door. A moment later, I was out onto the street, soaking in the taste of fumes and dust.

I hailed a musty looking Cab and asked the friendly old driver to take me to the Courthouse. On the seat beside me lay a copy of the New Yorker. The first pages were full uninteresting drivel, but an article on the 13th page intrigued me.

It's All Well on Wall Street

We have rejoiced in the annual budget being kept down, in reducing taxes, and paying off the national debt because the influence of such action is felt in every home in the land. It has meant that the people not only have greater resources with which to provide themselves with food and clothing and shelter but also for the enjoyment of what was but lately considered the luxuries of the rich. We call these results prosperity. They have come because people have been willing to do their duty. They have refrained from waste; they have shunned extravagance. It would be unfortunate, however, if out of these results, the impression should be gained that it is the obligation of the Gov-

ernment to furnish the people with prosperity.

They are entitled to such an administration of their affairs as will give them every fair opportunity, but it should always be remembered that if there is to be prosperity, they must furnish it for themselves. It all depends upon what use is made of the rewards of success. It is always possible to use them extravagantly and in disreputable ways. It is also possible to use them as the main supports of the real progress of enlightened civilization.

Prosperity is only an instrument to be used, not a deity to be worshiped. The industry and trade of the United States in 1921 were suffering from a grave recession. They had been severely affected by the inevitable reaction from the war period. Our foreign trade was experiencing a great decline. Production had been sharply restricted. There is a striking contrast between those dark days of 1921 and the remarkably favorable position of our trade and industry today. It

is the human element in the situation that deserves to be stressed first, and here the question of unemployment comes strongly to the front. In July 1921, more than 5,700,000 people were without work in the United States. At the present time, according to the most careful computation by the Department of
Labour, the number is not much more than 1,800,000, nearly half of whom are normally to be expected as temporarily unemployed while in transit from one position to another.

As a nation, we came out of the war with great losses. We made no profits from it. The apparent increases in wages were fictitious. We were poorer as a nation when we emerged from it. Yet during these last nine years, we have recovered from these losses and increased our national income by over one third even after discounting the inflation of the dollar. While some individuals have grown rich, there has also been a wide diffusion of our gain in wealth and income is marked and this is marked by a hundred proofs. I know of no better test of the improved conditions of the average family than the combined increase of life and industrial insurance, building and loan assets, and savings deposits. These are the financial agents of the average man. These alone have in seven years increased by nearly 100 percent to the gigantic sum of over fifty billions of dollars or nearly one-sixth of our whole national wealth. Today there are almost nine automobiles for every ten families, where seven and a half years ago only enough automobiles were running to average less than four for every ten families. The measure of progress is changing from the full dinner plate to the full garage. Our people have more to eat, better things to wear, and better homes. We have decreased the fear of old age, the fear of poverty, the fear of unemployment and these are fears which have always been amongst the greatest calamities of humankind.

I do not need to recite more figures and more evidence. There is not a person across the world that does not know the profound progress which our country has made in this period. Every man and woman know that their comfort, their hopes and their confidence for the future are higher this day than they were nine years ago.

I knew the article from the other day was a bunch of crap. This proved it. To be honest, I kind of depressed me that I was taking my money out. I felt as if I was losing out in the long run. But it'll be worth it. If it wasn't then I wouldn't do it.

While driving through New York towards the courthouse, the colonial mansions and brownstone houses lined my vision. The ladies on the street walked with a grace afforded to them by their husbands' jobs. I don't like these neighbourhoods. They stink of prejudice and familial dynasty, the side of New York I hate. The endlessly beautiful homes and archetypally English styling is pleasant to look at, but what lies beneath are labyrinths of cut-throat behavior and unpleasant rivalries. The streets may be lined with green trees and the gardens with exotic European flowers, but those are the only natural things that lie within the invisible walls of these neighborhoods.

We breezed through these streets quickly, they don't take up much of the city anymore, into a more modern setting. We were near the
West Village, a place where buildings emerged from the hard work and earnings of decent New York. I prefer it here. It doesn't stink of elitism but smells of success. Its beauty is built from the hardwork of its residents and not from the illicit earnings of relations from a century gone by. Places like this make me love New York, even if the rest of the world fails to see its beauty.

When New York is successful, people tar it as a citadel of inequality. Yet, really, it's simply a place where determination can be sometimes exchanged for destiny. Similarly, when it doesn't thrive, it's a cesspool of hopelessness. It's just not true as the residents of Manhattan are, to a large extent, strangers who have pulled up stakes somewhere and come to town, seeking sanctuary or fulfillment or some greater or lesser grail. The capacity to make such dubious gifts is a mysterious quality of New York. It can destroy an individual, or it can fulfill them, depending on a good deal on luck. No one should come to New York to live unless they are willing to be lucky. But does this make it a bad place? That's not for me to decide, but I'm sure you know my verdict.

Eventually, the dirty old cab pulled up to the curb beside the courthouse. After paying the driver, I turned around to face the mountain of stone and mortar authority that lay before me.

The courthouse itself is a very grand building. Fourteen pillars hold up a triangular stone carving of our founding fathers. The front door stands five people tall with stone slabs all around it. The greyness of the sky almost made the detail at the back of the building indiscernible, but I could spot the Roman style windows along the side walls. Trees surrounded the edge of the building on either side clearly placed as mere decorations. The gleaming courthouse was a relatively new addition to the city, and its grandeur stood out from the mass of nondescript buildings surrounding it. The pillars were unbreakable and its intimidating presence undeniable. No matter the man, everyone feels small stood before its steps.

I climbed them two at a time, overtaking causal bystanders and dawdling officials on my way. I stopped just before the door... took a very large breath, and proceeded in. My shoes clicked against the black and white marble floors, echoing off the stone walls. The hall was hexagonal and has five different archways. I didn't need to consider which one I needed to follow as the littering of people from the one in the corner of my eye gave me the answer. I dodged the people and headed through the archway; I was led to a swerving staircase encased with a white marble handrail. I followed the stairs upwards and eventually found the courtroom. It was as I expected. Walls lined the walnut stands, and the shined marble floors took the attention from the four chandeliers ranked in a square formation. The floor to ceiling windows were dressed with deep purple curtains that were identical in color to the padded velvet seats that wrapped around in a semicircle, all facing the judges seat. To my surprise, I found Stuart Thorsby, an old partner from the firm, and Elliot on the other side of the doorway. In fact, the room was filled with faces from the firm. Stuart looked at me in a confused fashion, and Elliot smirked at me. My urges to punch Elliot in the face were subdued by Stuarts questioning.

"John, whatever are you doing here?
You aren't part of this case." I was momentarily very confused as to why I was in the wrong room, then I realized. This is the room for the flagship case. My mind froze, and I gave them a blank look, god, I must have looked stupid. Eventually, I fumbled a response.
"Well I, erm, I have, I, I just came to wish you luck on your case."
Elliot's smirk grew even wider, and Stuart looked at me with bemusement. I wanted the floor to fall through, I felt as if years of building up my reputation within the partners as a professional, smart lawyer had crumbled. I was reduced to being the boy that was caned by his headmaster again.

Then Stuart finally replied. "Well, that's

awful nice of you, John. But we've got a case to get on with and well, so do you."

"Right, yes, thanks" Mr. Thorsby, "I'll do just that." As I turned towards the door, the already deep blade was twisted by Elliot. "Good luck Jonny boy, and with the judge you've got, you'll need it." The arrogant amusement he carried was by no means hidden. I wanted to give him a piece of my mind, but I kept on walking, he's just not worth it.

Eventually, I found our courtroom. It took me a while. I guess I wasn't aware they had courtrooms in the basement. Officials jostled in front of the closed door, the courtroom had yet to be opened. I spotted Chauncey in the corner, talking with his wife in serious undertones. The atmosphere was relatively relaxed, there were a few people in small groups chatting about unimportant matters.

I spotted the prosecution lawyer, Newland Mason. He stood with his back leaning on the wall. His body was lean, he had a square jaw and short, dark hair with bags under his eyes and a suit which clearly had been put on before he began his overnight preparations for the case. He stood quietly with a cream-colored case file in his hand, his black leather briefcase beside him on the floor.

Soon enough, the clerk arrived, his metal keys jangling through the sudden anticipation in the hall to unlock the heavy door. Suddenly the once relaxed characters turned into a swarm of angered bees, the general chatter had given away to a cascade of people rushing in to find their place in the proceedings.

Considering the building was new, courtroom was squalid and unadorned and dirty. It gave off a sense of abandonment and belied the passing of rosier times. Once white walls were smeared in certain places, the light funnels were doing their best, but the basement room was unashamedly a very dark place to be. The chairs were clean but had been torn in many places. Behind the judges' chair, a crucifix with the words “The Law is equal for all” was present. In the corner, a faded American flag stood proudly. I found my seat and spread out my files, trying to look as composed as possible.

Then Chauncey sauntered in. He wore a grey suit with a black tie and white shirt. He was severely overweight. His years of indulgence had clearly caught up with him. Nobody would have guessed he remained in his late thirties.

He gave a huge sigh, offering a whiff of his tobacco laden breath in the process. “So where’s the girl?” He asked. “They not allowed in here or something” he laughed at his blatantly unfunny remark, so I didn’t have to. “No, well I think we can win this case between us
Chauncey, their case relies on the fact that the company knew nothing of the illicit

actions, so as long as we can prove that they knew –“

“Sounds good to me, John.”

“Are you sure?”

“Completely.”

Everyone seemed to be in place and ready to proceed. The Courtroom was rather small, but somehow a good audience had amassed, to the extent a few had to stand at the back. Some people looked a little misplaced. Chauncey's family and friends sat on one side behind a row of reporters. They sat nervously. His wife was all dressed up for the occasion with a plunged cream dress that fitted her a long while ago, while what I assumed to be his mother wore a simple black jumper with a reserved neckline.

They sat watching the room tentatively, trying to avoid eye contact with the mass of reporters on the other side of the benches. There were clumps of them all peering their beady eyes around the room like hawks, treating a good story as their prey.

A scrawny looking Clerk of no more than twenty stood up and attempted to garner everyone's attention, he was ignored for the large part but after a minute or so the general chatter subsided.

"Hello everyone, we are ready to begin, but unfortunately the judge is running about fifteen minutes late so we'll have to be patient until he arrives." He stood down very quickly, and everyone returned to their conversations. I talked with Chauncey about his testimony and talked him through what to do and what not to do. He appeared to be listening, yet his mind was too full of worry, I couldn't help but notice his sweaty palms and his foot tapping. I guess the apparently confident man of moments ago was now gone.

Then the door's latch lifted, and it swung

open, as if in slow motion. The room's darkness was lifted momentarily as the light from the hall spread to all corners of the room. In from it walked a slim figure. She wore a bright blue dress, with white heels and a cream coat. In one hand she held a file and on the other a small purse. She had short hair that framed her face and gave a slight grin on satisfaction when everyone looked at her. The whole room watched her as she walked down the aisle. They knew she wasn't a judge, but she wasn't a reporter or spectator either, she had too much of a purpose. It didn't matter either way. I knew exactly who she was.

She reached the front and sat down next to me, put her bag down, and turned to me. "Did I miss anything?" she asked. "Rosalie, what are you doing here? I replied.
"Well, my job." She answered.

I was all kinds of confused. This morning she had quit the firm, or so I had thought.

Then right before the start of court, she turns up, blowing through the door like a leaf in the wind as if nothing happened. As if Elliot didn't happen. She was acting crazy.

Chauncey was sat there, not knowing what to say, or do, or most likely think for that matter. Rosalie leaned over me and took his hand to shake. "I don't believe we've met in person, I'm Rosalie." He looked right through her and replied, "Well, it's nice to meet you and all, and it was good of you to come, but well, you won't be representing me will you?" He asked. Looking a little confused, she retorted, "Well, of course, I will. There was a tense moment that followed, it may have been silent, but a thousand words were being conveyed." Look, Rosalie? Is it? You cannot just turn up here late, after having been incompetent for an entire week on the telephone and expect to just take control of the case when the reality is you aren't even suited to this line of work."

It was a pretty direct way of putting it.

Rosalie's eyes became fierce, and her face tense. "So, actually, I'm not late as I haven't seen court start yet, have you? And in terms of incompetence, I have built the backbone of your defense, I have rung you five times a day for the one time you'd pick up, and I was telling you everything perfectly fine on the telephone, you just don't want to hear from anyone of the opposite sex. Now I would really appreciate it if you could sit back and allow me to do my job."
That was an even more direct way of putting it.

Chauncey's pride had clearly been damaged, but still, he tried to combat her. "Listen here, I don't know who you think you are but –" Once again the latch lifted and the door swung open.

In walked the judge. The chatter fell silent. The judge was a very tall, elderly man. The bailiff stood up and shouted, "all rise for the court" in an authoritative tone. Everybody immediately stood up. The Bailiff continued. "Hear ye, hear ye, the criminal court for the eleventh district is now in session, the honorable Clarence Dangerfield presiding. Let all matters come forth. May God bless this court."

I looked at Rosalie. Her face had become white, and her hands tightened around the piece paper she was holding. Out of all the judges in New York, this is the one we were given. I wasn't sure what
Rosalie was going to do. It must have taken a lot to get her here, I wouldn't have been surprised if she'd have ditched if I'm honest. I wouldn't have blamed her.

Judge Dangerfield, with his seemingly endless black robe flowing behind him, took his place behind the elevated bench and said, "please be seated." I glanced around. There wasn't an empty seat anywhere. I knew the feeling people had of the trial. There was a feeling amongst those who know that Chauncey was going down. It was thought he would afford some decent lawyers that could punch holes in the prosecution and attempt to redirect the blame to another source, but then eventually Chauncey would be put away with no damage to the firm he was a part of.

Judge Dangerfield instructed the Bailiff to bring in the jury. A door opened, and the courtroom was still as the jurors filed in and filled the jury box. Everyone watched them closely as they took their seats and settled in. Unsurprisingly I recognized none of them. Most looked like they didn't want to be there, though there were a few elderly ones that looked glad to be out of the house.

Dangerfield quizzed them for a few minutes. He was just making sure none of them had improper contact. It's pretty much just a formality. Judges always ask them, and jurors always say no.

Soon enough, prosecutor Mason stood up.

He got straight into the case, acting rather abruptly in the process. He kept on using phrases like "if we look at the facts" and "the facts imply this." For the most part, the first ten or so minutes of his ramble was a rehashing of the facts everyone already knew. Nothing we weren't expecting. Then he got a little more heated.

"The motive was simply money. Mr. Chauncey embezzled the hard-earned money of our fellow American citizens who knew no better than to trust him." He took a dramatic water break mid-sentence. I'm pretty sure Rosalie rolled her eyes. Then he continued. "He then hid them in since disposed of accounts within the firm. He did this of his own accord. Fact. He did this with money he was supposed to invest for his clients. Fact. He used the firm Lockton and Horby to facilitate his own illicit deals. Fact. He is guilty of all that he is accused. Fact."

With great drama, the jurors absorbed

every word. The courtroom was deadly silent, and Newland stepped closer to the jury. “This was a crime against the good and honest, to serve the corrupt and greedy. This man knew exactly what he was doing, and I am in no doubt he would do it again”. Newland Mason proceeded to sit down, at that moment, I could not imagine there was a single person in the courtroom who believed Chauncey was innocent.

Judge Dangerfield tapped his gavel and called for a fifteen-minute recess.
Moving almost faster than I could comprehend, Rosalie stood up and rocketed out of the room. Telling me she had an idea.

I was in a state of panic. The prosecution had come out strong, stronger than I’d anticipated. They’d foreseen our angle of redirecting blame to the firm and derailed it with their opening remark. Rosalie needed a trick up her sleeve.

Precisely fifteen minutes later, everyone was back in place. Judge Dangerfield took his seat and asked for the defense to make their opening statement. Rosalie stood up slowly and walked towards the small podium in front of the jury. I could immediately hear murmuring from around the room. The prosecution was both shocked and amused; even the judge appeared to be a little more intrigued. There was shocked murmuring as she walked forward in front of the jury box. Judge Dangerfield seemed mildly amused, Rosalie seemed mildly petrified. Though I don't think anyone but me realized this. Then she began. Starting with a pleasant "Good morning, ladies and gentlemen of the jury." She then introduced herself and then pointed at Chauncey and me introducing us too.

Rosalie stood tall on the podium, I could tell she was petrified, but she was hiding it well if you didn't know her. Everyone was in shock still, but Rosalie did a good job of breaking the ice and explaining her job. I guess like me everyone had heard of women going into jobs like this, but nobody had seen it yet. Rosalie went on the counter much of Mason's argument. Poking holes in his assumptions and spinning around points to be in our favor. Then she went for the kill.

"The truth is, Chauncey is not the criminal. He is the fall guy. The fall guy for an operation that runs throughout the entire company. He was simply an errand boy, used as a vehicle to move money from good, trusting Americans into the banks of sleazy executives. Do you want to know the reason the prosecution claims the money Chauncey allegedly stole to be untraceable? Because there isn't money to trace. At least not to Chauncey anyway. That money is long gone, it has become a pebble in the mountain of illgotten gains owned by Wall Street elites. Chauncey did not know he was transferring the money into the wrong accounts. He was simply told what to do, and he did it. In fact, Chauncey did not even open the accounts in which the money was stored. There is documentation from J.P Morgan, proving it was the president of acquisitions Mr. Arnold Wallstein that opened the accounts. Thus, proving that the documentation given to the police by Lockton and Horby is, in fact, fraudulent suggesting Mr. Chauncey was set up to cover up some vile financial crimes which, if Mr. Chauncey is found guilty, will be locked away with him. The prosecution would like you to believe that Mr. Chauncey, a hardworking, good-natured family man is guilty so that the true criminals can be protected. But ladies and gentlemen of the jury, this will be history repeating itself. Four years ago, Lockton and Horby found themselves in the same position. A young man had allegedly stolen funds from numerous family wills and donation pools and embezzled it with an account he opened under the firms' name. He was imprisoned for two years. Eight years ago, a man from the firm apparently stole money from families across Ohio, claiming to them that they'd invested in a Chemical manufacturing plant, he was locked away for six years. Yet, from all the money stolen, none of it was ever recovered. The state and the firm claim it must have been hidden away.

The link between those cases and the one lying before us today is undeniable. Just like then, a lone wolf is claimed to be responsible for an operation that would require the aid of a small team to work properly. The money is said to have miraculously disappeared, just like before. If we all fall for it, the firm is once again in the clear, using an innocent man who didn't know any better to face the charges, so they don't have to. I cannot tell you exactly who within the firm is responsible for these crimes. But I can tell you it was not my client. It was not Mr. Chauncey."

She looked into the eyes of the jury members, then across to the prosecution table. Then she sat down.

The courtroom was jolted, Rosalie had just come out with evidence nobody was expecting, least of all the prosecution, least of all me. Newland Mason stood up and walked over to the judge. They spoke intently for a few moments, and then he went to sit down. Rosalie was then called over to the judge.

The tension in the courtroom was stifling. Nobody spoke. The ticking of the clock was very clear. The faint whispers of Rosalie and Judge Dangerfield echoed around the room. Everybody wanted to hear what was being said, but it was impossible to tell. The scrawny looking clerk was then called over, adding further intensity to the room. Rosalie then walked over to me with a look of vague satisfaction.

"The evidence is allowed to stand if we can provide the paperwork and a witness from the bank that dealt with the firm".

"Well can we do all those things?" "Yes, we can. I have the paperwork proving who opened the account with me here." She pulled out some cream papers with an embossed stamp and ink signature. "However, I need to run down to the bank and get my witness, I didn't know I'd need him so soon. If we can get him this trial could be over today." I was not expecting it to be over so quickly, but equally, I liked the idea of getting out of there, as long as we won. "John, the only issue is that while I'm gone, you will need to do the cross-examination of the detective. Are you fine doing that?"

I thought I was doing that anyway.

"Yes, Yes I'm fine to do that Rosalie. You go get our witness." She picked up her bag and coat, turning around to leave. Before she left our table though, she turned back around. "Oh, and Jonny," she asked.

"Yes," I replied. "Stick by the book, the judge runs a tight courtroom and is looking for a chance to trip us over." He didn't like me pulling that evidence, and I think he has a predisposition against us. I mean, when he with spoke to me he just looked through me. I had to use court protocol to my favor so that I could bypass him and leave to the courtroom." With that, she whisked off and out of the courtroom with a hurried grace.

Before I could cross-examine of their witness, the prosecution would get their turn with Chauncey. He was looking a little rosier after Rosalie's surprise evidence had come to light. The prosecution table had been manic, but it's was a little late in the game for them to come back unless they had a surprise witness of their own.

Newland Mason cross-examined Chauncey and tried to beat him up a little. Sure, there were some cracks in his defense, but Mason didn't get anything new on him. Chauncey stuck to his story and Mason did the same. Like all good prosecutors, and it pains me to say that Mason was one, he was slow and methodical. Nonetheless, after over an hour, he began to repeat the same questions that warranted the same answers. I began to object but the judge was firmly not on our side and was clearly in no hurry; he was trying to buy the prosecution time. Another fifteen minute recess was called, after that, I would have my turn to pick apart the detective.

Though most of the audience wouldn't admit it, they appeared to be getting bored. It was almost three P.M. Many of them saw the trial going in a certain direction. To many the ruling was just an inevitability. The truth is as long as Rosalie returned with our witness we were in the clear and Chauncey was free.

I began my cross-examination of the detective with some simple questions. I established the facts and gaged the detective's stance on the case. I asked him if it was reasonable to suggest one man could fool an entire company, numerous investors, and seamlessly embezzle money for over a year without anyone noticing. Yes, it was reasonable apparently. While there were no traces left, nobody saw anything, and little was suspected of Chauncey throughout the time. The detective stood by the fact he had been doing it alone, without the knowledge of the company.

“So, you are certain it was Chauncey?" I asked.

“Yes, it's the only plausible answer.” He replied. Unknown to the detective, that slip up gave me an opening.

“Oh, so your entire argument is based on plausibility detective?”
“No, I am merely – “
“Because it would be entirely plausible that there were more people involved than just Mr. Chauncey would it not?”
“Well, yes, I suppose it would.” “It could

be entirely plausible that we are helping to cover the tracks for an operation bigger than we know."

"Well hold on for a second now - I raised my voice above his. "It could be entirely plausible that Mr. Chauncey has been set up, could it not detective?" He seemed speechless. The courtroom had lost its boredom, that was for sure.

"Now, I believe you are stretching the evidence there my boy." The detective had moved past being agitated. He was borderline furious.

"No detective, the evidence has been stretched to fit a crime my client simply did not commit."

I paused before attacking him again "So you say you are sure my client is guilty?" I asked. "The evidence given to me suggests that Mr. Chauncey is, in fact, guilty." Well I suppose you are an experienced officer, aren't you, detective?" I inquired. "Yes, I have served for just over twenty-five years...." So just how many financial crime cases like this have you investigated?" I questioned. He looked at me, blankly, "I do not specialize in financial crimes." I couldn't help but smile. "There we have it, you, the detective, claim to believe the evidence suggests that my client is guilty. Yet judging from your experience you wouldn't know a financial crime if it ran across the road in front of you." The jury soaked up every word I said. The judge gave me a warning, but the damage had been done, their only credible witness had no credibility.

The cross-examination quickly spiraled downwards. We both got angry. He continuously interrupted me. The judge barked back and forth at us, but the fight was on.
The fact of the matter was the detective admitted too much. He admitted he hadn't much experience and wasn't interested in the financial sector. He admitted he didn't know how Chauncey could have hidden the money. By the end of it, he

admitted it wouldn't be certain Chauncey was guilty. The longer we argued, the worse he looked, I scored points by pecking away at his testimony. Finally, after an hour of brutal questioning, I said I was finished.

When I turned away from the jury box, I saw Rosalie had returned, her witness in tow. I sat back down, and we were given five minutes to prep, not that we needed it at that point. The witness was about my age, smartly dressed, plain-looking. He was called Jack Barley. You know the type. When he was called up, Mason did his best to tear him down. Barley wasn't the most confident nor the most persuasive, but he didn't have to be. His story was simple, believable, and true. Through the short questioning period, Mason did more damage to his case than anything else. The truth was Jack Barley had no reason to lie, no motive beyond being a decent person, and the jury knew that.

We were given an hour's recess while the

decisions were being made, so we had some food at the restaurant across from the courthouse. Chauncey was a picture of arrogance, suddenly he thought the world of Rosalie claiming he "never doubted her." I didn't want to tempt fate and celebrate early, but that didn't stop Chauncey. In my experience, sometimes a jury can be unpredictable, especially when a firm with big money behind them is involved in the situation. When we arrived back at the courtroom, everyone was talking at once, the reasonably sized room buzzed with anticipation. As we Lawyers appeared from the back, people took their seat. All eyes were on Mr. Chauncey as he walked to his chair, he offered a nervous smile, the arrogant man from the restaurant had disappeared before the courtroom's eyes.

The bailiff waited until all were settled, then yelled, "All rise for the court." We all jumped to our feet as Judge Dangerfield appeared through the rear door, his long black cloak and young Legal clerk tracing behind him. I looked up to see everyone standing for him out of respect, I decided in that instant that being a judge wouldn't be all that bad. At least people seemed to respect you.

Judge Dangerfield lowered himself into his wooden throne and said: "please be seated." The crowd fell noisily onto the benches. The Judge then asked, "please bring in the jury." It took an eternity to get the jury seated, but finally, the old woman who got lost on her way to the toilet made it back to her seat. The foreman of the jury walked over to the stand and spoke. "Moments ago, a decision was made by the jury in relation to the fate of Charles Chauncey. On the charge of embezzlement, Charles Chauncey is found not guilty. On the charge of fraud ... Charles Chauncey is also found ... not guilty."

I let out a huge sigh of relief. Chauncey's

smile was undeniable. His wife jumped from her chair. Newland Mason's hand smashed against the table. All the while, Judge Dangerfield banged his gavel and declared "Court adjourned." All of a sudden, Chauncey was swarmed by reporters. Rosalie and I slipped out of the side door. When we were out of the door, she thanked me for persuading her to stay. I think winning the case and coming out with a secret witness gave her some newfound confidence. As she walked out of the courthouse, there was an undeniable spring in her step.

I had to wait around for a little while. Nobody had spoken to Chauncey about paying for our fees, and we don't come cheap. I rounded the corner, passing Newland Mason in the process. He offered me a filthy look, but deep down I think he wanted to cry. The calm, collected smart man that walked into the courthouse this morning had gone. The one leaving looked unsure of himself, angry and rather frustrated. To think that could have been me.

After rounding the corner, I spotted Chauncey. He was talking intimately with his wife. I'm no eavesdropper, but I couldn't help but overhear them. "Listen, I know you got away with it this time but you've gotta be more careful. If it wasn't for those fancy lawyers, you'd have been toast." The wife was speaking in hushed tones, but I caught every word. I couldn't believe what I was hearing. Then Chauncey said, "I know baby, I'm gonna get my act together. No more of that illegal bullshit. I'm going straight. I, I promise. But first I'm gonna have to find a new job." His wife looked at him sternly.

"You'd better, we've got little Julian to think about now, he don't need no Daddy in prison, but he don't need no Daddy out of work neither." Chauncey looked a little lost for words.

"I know, I know. But I can hardly go back to work, can I? We were all in it together, and they just dumped the blame on me.

They'll get caught sooner or later. Come on lets go home." I didn't have the appetite to speak to him. I genuinely thought he was innocent of all of it. I had sat in that courtroom and defended a guilty man to the end of the earth. I had prepared relentlessly to help him. I possibly ruined Newland Mason's career for him, and Chauncey was nothing but a lousy liar. A lousy liar who stole from the innocent to feed the rich. I'd just been a cog in their machine of injustice. I didn't know that then. I know that now.

Winning the case made me look good, but it made me feel like crap. I thought I'd figured it out, but I was taken for a fool, what's the point in any of it. I can be a partner. I can live in a fancy apartment and buy my wife nice clothes. I can have everyone in the courtroom stand for me and listen to every word I utter. I can have my name known by anyone worth my time. I can be the best lawyer money can buy. I can do all of that. But if I can't tell innocent from

guilty. Good from the bad.
Right from wrong. If I can't do the right thing when the right needs to be done, then what's the point?

CHAPTER FIVE

It was that same evening when my wife and I went out to celebrate. I really didn't feel like partying, but she was excited and I didn't have the heart to tell her I'd defended a crook. I didn't have the heart to tell anyone. I couldn't really drink much as I had my partnership interview the next morning. That kind of annoyed me. I was in the mood to forget who I am for a night.

The bar was bursting at the seams. The whole of New York seemed to have come out tonight. There was a mass of people wearing shiny, cone-shaped hats. They all danced without a care in the world. A few of us more solemn guys sat around the bar. I hadn't been to that bar before, but it was very nice. The ceiling was shaped in an arch and had was painted to look like the sky. Little angels and doves were detailed on one side while bright, dream-like clouds filled the other side of the painting. I'd never seen anything like it. It almost seemed too angelic, too pure to be looking over a bar. But maybe that was the point. On the other side of the room, there was a mural that covered the entirety of the wall. It was a painting of Venice. The focus of the painting was the river and the calm sunset beating down onto it. On the side of the river there were old men sitting outside a restaurant, drinking wine and smoking cigars and reminiscing. It was a very peaceful setting. On the other side, there was a darker theme however. A young boy was drowning in the river, he was drowning in plain sight. Nobody seemed to be looking though, nobody was there to save him.

It was again, an odd piece to have in a

bar, but I still appreciated the artistic attempts the owner had made. Aside from the decoration, the architecture of the bar was magnificent. Unlike the basement courtroom I'd spent the day in, this basement had ceilings four people high, symmetrical pillars upholding the ceilings we lay under and stonework fit for a palace. My wife had gone off with her sister dancing, but I remained at the bar. In a room full of people, it was a lonely place to be. The other guys sitting around me were clearly on the tail end of a rough day. Most had come straight from work as their tired suits, and loose ties would tell you. Then I spotted someone I knew, or at least I thought I did, he did look very different from when I knew him. He had swept back hair and a greying beard that had massively outgrown him. His face moved into his neck, and he carried a scar running along with his left cheek. It had faded since I'd last seen him. He stood out a little from the men around him. Partially due to

his tall, broad stature, partially due to his clothing. Unlike the black and grey suits around him. His was a dark beige suit, wearing it with a pink shirt and patterned burgundy tie. I certainly recognized him, but I doubt he recognized me.
His name was Mr. Irrumator, and I worked for him a good deal of time ago. I was a fresh graduate from Columbia's law school. He was my first boss at my first job. I worked there for around two years in total. It was the firm I was at to before I found where I am now.
Anyway, I worked closely with Mr. Irrumator and put everything into the job. I spent my weekends networking, I put in masses of overtime. I went above and beyond, not because I had to, I enjoyed it if I'm honest. I was good at it. One day Mr. Irrumator came into the office and announced that a huge trial was coming up and he would be taking on one junior lawyer to help assist him. It was a big deal, everyone in the city talked about the case.

I knew I had to get the job.

I think the big difference between myself and the other junior lawyers was that I spoke up. They were always quiet and obedient. Doing what was asked when it was asked of them, but that wasn't me. I questioned the senior lawyers, I tested them, and I tried to make myself better. I thought it was a good thing. I'd always seen it that way. Anyway, so when it came down to getting the job, I thought I had a great shot.

I tried to be a good lawyer throughout my time there, whereas many of the other guys only buckled down when they clocked onto Mr. Irrumator's prize. I hoped he'd know that. Suddenly everyone was working overtime, everyone was talking to him any chance they got. I didn't do that. I refused to suck up. While we didn't talk too often, I gaged there was a level of mutual respect there, so I didn't feel the need to. I knew my merit would get me there. That's what I hoped. Boy was I wrong.

It came down to the evening before the decision was made. I was pretty tense, I'd been told by another partner that the interview I had was "outstanding," but I had a gut feeling something was up. I ended up hearing early that I didn't get the job. The guy who did leaked it, so it was common knowledge by the time of the announcement the next day. I really liked the guy who got it, we were good friends and had a lot in common. He didn't question as much as me. He never drew attention to himself, never did anything particularly wrong, but nothing particularly right either.

I felt as though Mr. Irrumator picked someone who would extend his ideas, not offer new ones. After that ordeal I didn't really want to work there. I had signed to work there for three years but when I asked to be relieved things got nasty. I was labeled ungrateful, self-entitled, arrogant, but the truth is I was none of those things. I am none of those things. Perhaps I was the only one who saw my hard work. Wouldn't surprise me. Mr. Irrumator wouldn't let me go and became an ass. We didn't often talk before, but he blanked completely after it all went down. He walked past me in the hall without a greeting. Looked right through me if I asked him a question. Yet he still expected me to serve the firm as I did before. I was expected to continue on as if they hadn't kicked me in the teeth and pushed me down the stairs. Instead, he just fired me. I think it was because of my "abrasive attitude and entitled behavior." I can't really remember but what I did, but it didn't warrant that. I got a new job at a better firm soon after and forgot about it.

The only thing I know is that Mr. Irrumator ended up losing the case.
It was very public. I read somewhere that he was made to resign and hasn't been pre-

sent in the legal world since. I felt bad for him to an extent, he was so obsessed with building up the firms prestige that he took the soul of out the place, then his job went and took the soul out of him. He focused so much on reputation and being saleable that he stopped being good at his job. Now all he has is a very public failure to show for it. All the while, I was doing better than ever, reading about the chaos from the comfort of my new job, with more prospects and potential than he could have ever given me. It's funny how life works out sometimes.

I watched him sitting at the bar. I didn't resent him anymore. I never had really. Watching him sitting there, alcohol as his only company,

I realized he did me a favor. I didn't have to spend a year working on that deathtrap of a case that would have cost my career. Instead, I focused on my marriage, on more interesting work, on becoming better. I guess that's why I am so hungry for my promotion now. I know my worth, and I know I should be a partner, so I will be. I won't be hard done by this time.

I stood up and walked over to him. Up close, I could see he had put on some weight. His face was pale, but he had red puffed up cheeks and redness surrounding his eyes. I introduced myself. "Hi Mr. Irrumator, I'm John, I worked for you a few years back now." He looked at me squarely, he no longer looked through me, he hadn't the right to. "Yes, I remember you... I fired you if I remember correctly. Sorry about that, it was nothing personal." His voice had become much crokier since I'd last spoke to him, it had lost its life a little bit. Then he continued "and call me Jack, I ain't your boss anymore. I'm nobody's boss." He turned away from me back to the company of his whiskey. I didn't see the point in continuing the conversation, so I just went back to my seat across the bar, I shouldn't have bothered. By then, the dancefloor had tired my wife out, we strolled back home through the city. The crisp air absorbed momentarily absorbed all of my worries and doubts. Suddenly the shame of freeing a guilty man lessened and the worry of not being good enough faded. If there's one thing seeing Jack Irrumator showed me, it is that nobody's success is infinite, so I should enjoy it while it lasts.

CHAPTER SIX

The next morning my wife woke me up with a plate of eggs and some juice. She thought coffee could make my breath smell for the interview. I put on my favorite white shirt and lucky red tie. The one I wore on my interview to Columbia all those years ago.

As I was running quite early, I stepped onto the balcony to take a moment. The sun was rising, illuminating the skyline and giving the city life again. Workmen were still trying to fix the stock brokerage advertisement. Usually, they are up down and out, but this time they'd been up there a few mornings this week, maybe they were just being lazy. Wouldn't surprise me. I wanted to have a quiet moment but the city was too awake for that. I walked back through my room to leave, and I noticed the platinum green wallpaper was nearly falling off the wall entirely by this point. I asked my wife about it, and she told me she'd tried to make it stick back on, but nothing was working. I swear, all these fancy modern things are too good to be true, none of them ever work. I left early and so arrived at 08:20. The walk through the city was pleasant, and I made good time, it wasn't as interesting as the day before but I guess I didn't want it to be. I didn't want anything else on my mind.

I walked into work to find the place was thriving. People were hugging, shouting, clapping, and jumping. I was back in kindergarten again. I spotted Rosalie in the corner and paced over to her to see what's going on.

As I was walking over, I caught the eyes of a few people. None of them looked at me differently. They all looked at me like they had the past four years I'd been an associate. It was as if I wasn't the man who'd won the case for Chauncey. The man who'd defeated reputable prosecutor Newland Mason. The man who was about become a partner.

I asked Rosalie what was going on and she looked at me in disbelief.

"Haven't you heard? They won the flagship case. The legal world's been shaken upside down. Everyone's going crazy." I couldn't believe it, that case was a tough one to crack. We were defending a crime syndicate so brutally deadly the police refused to infiltrate them. How we won is beyond me; I really question the justice system sometimes.

"That's, that's amazing. Has anyone heard about our trial then?" I didn't want to sound desperate for attention, so I acted casual when asking her. She looked at me and just laughed.

"Jonny, nobody cares about us defending the freedom of a nobody like Chauncey when the firm has just won the biggest case of the last decade." I think she could see the disappointment on my face as her next words were a little kinder. "Look, John, we know we won and that's enough. You can't let this stupid thing get in your head right before the interview. You've gotta focus. And speaking of which you've gotta go, the interview starts in ten minutes.

I felt deflated. All of our hard work and excellence had been overshadowed. What I thought could have been a competitive edge going into my interview probably wasn't even known by the partners. I went into the waiting room outside the senior partner's office. It was a very nice area with a plush burgundy carpet and windows overlooking the street and books on shelves covering the walls. There were about eight other guys sat waiting too. I guess I wasn't the only one who thought it would look good to get there early. I was certainly on the younger side out of the guys sitting around me. I knew all of them, many worked on my floor. I even recognized a guy who went to college with me, though it wasn't the time to bring any of that up. One by one, everyone was called in, chewed up, and spat back out. I was the last one to go in. Even though I had a plan to make sure I was going to get the job, I was still so nervous. What if they thought I was so bad the money coming there way didn't make a difference? There were a hundered things that could go wrong, all standing in the way of what needs to go right. I need this promotion. I need it for my marriage. To show Mr. Irrumator. To show my father. To show everyone who doubted me, I needed it so badly it hurt.

Finally, my name was called. Suddenly my legs ceased up. My mouth ran dry. Sure, I had the money backing me, but at that point it meant nothing. I wasn't thinking straight, I know that now. As I walked towards the door, I could feel my heart pumping. Somehow my body walked towards the door even though every part of my head was telling me to run. Then suddenly I was in an oak-panelled room facing two elderly partners who were ready to either tear me apart or build me up stronger. That part was up to them. The door closed, and all I heard was "Good morning young man, please take a seat."

I thought the interview went well.

Perhaps there were some things I could have phrased better or some answers that could have been more thorough. It worried me that they didn't bring up my courtroom victory and only focused on my earlier works, some of which are impressive, some not so much. Realistically, as long as I got the money to Mark, it would be fine. The decision was set to come out either in a day or so after the interview. They just need the money before then.

I've heard of the process before I spoke

with Mark. Lots of people do it. Basically, Mark is in contact with senior officials in companies who want to earn some extra money on the side. I send my money to Mark, who takes a small amount for himself. The rest is given to the senior official. They tamper with the decision by changing CV's or something like that. Then ure enough, after a couple of days, the payer is given a promotion, and the officials pockets are lined. Senior corporate figures and partners do it for the extra income because half the time they aren't bothered with who gets a promotion anyway. Some may call it unethical, but I've come to realize the lines between what's right and what's sensible are blurred to the point that your conscience has you walking around in dazed circles. Besides, everyone has to get their hands dirty once in a while.

I didn't really have much to do at work, so I left early and took a walked back. The sun was already setting on the

city, creating bronze shadows from grey bricks.
The sky was filled with dark, heavy clouds blocking out the final shards of sunlight from touching the path in front of me. It may have been a dark walk, but I supposed that only made home feel warmer when I finally arrived home.

I came home to find my wife in the living room, trying on all of her new clothes. To me, they looked like more of the same but she insisted they were all of the highest fashion and completely necessary. I was sitting down, catching up on empty news articles as she paraded me with her recent purchases. The constant changing tired her out. She sat down next to me, reading her latest edition of socialite drivel. After I was done with my newspaper, I got back to worrying about the money, Mark, and the partners. Soon enough, I caved in and rang Marshal, just to check up more than anything. We went through the motions of me having to remind him who I was again, but eventually we got there and my identity was once again established.

"Don't worry John" he told me. "Everything's ready to go for tomorrow, Mr. Devlin will receive your funds in the morning." His usually smooth voice was terribly shaky, cracked in places. "Well ok," I replied, "I just wanted to –
""Listen John," he interjected. "I've got something going on right now, it's really crazy here. Can I call you back?"I was taken aback, his voice went from shaky to desperate. "Yes, that's ok. But please can you make sure you do call me back because – ".
The call went dead.
I was annoyed. He just cut me off. Even more so when I wasn't called back that evening. I got it, I really did. Sometimes I've been rung up by a client when I was busy, or something was going wrong, or I just didn't want to deal with them. I did understand how he felt completely.

I guess what I didn't understand was the feeling of being on the other side of the telephone.

After the line went dead and I'd contemplated my situation I walked back through and sat with my wife. "How did it go today?" She asked. Her eyes were filled with hope. My answer carried with it the promise of a new apartment in a nicer area, the possibility of new friends and the certainty of new clothes. "It erm, it went well. I'll be shocked if there's anything but good news for us over the next few days." I told her. Her face lit up a like a Ferris wheel, her eyes offering a sense of joy and relief. Then she replied. "That's so great darling, this promotion will do wonders for our marriage!" With that her head sunk onto my lap and her feet hung over the edge of the chair. She picked up some more socialite drivel and became lost in a world of superficial reality.

I sat there for a while, watching the ensuing storm outside build up its rage. Watching as the billboards wavered against the wind. I didn't know what to make of my wife's comment. I know to her saying things like that are meant senselessly, but to me they hurt. Did it mean she'd leave me if I didn't make partner? I dreaded to think. I stopped bothering to think altogether. A quote from my favorite Childhood story entered my head and set me to sleep – "what will be will be and what we don't know we'll see." With that, I fell asleep to the assurance my life was about to become better than even my childhood hopes had imagined.

CHAPTER SEVEN

I woke up to the sound of a huge crash.

My wife had fallen asleep on my lap so we were both just lying in the living room when it happened. I raced to the window. The rain was still pounding the other side of the glass, but I could still clearly see what had happened. The billboard advertising the stock brokerage had been thrown off the hinges that held it in place, falling ten floors down. The impact of the ground shattered the sign into a million pieces all over the road. The fallen sign revealed another, much smaller, less

outlandish sign. It was more of a banner really, and it hung on top of a small building. The banner stated "When it gets hard, God is the answer, when it's going easy God is the reason." It took me a moment to process what it was saying, and I didn't like it one bit. I wish I didn't have to look at that tripe out of my window. Religious values are so outdated. The huge crash had already woken me up, I watched as people from nearby building poured onto the street.
Eventually, the cops arrived at the scene looking pretty panicky. Soon after, a truck arrived, and men hopped off with barrels and containers to put all the broken pieces into so the road could be cleared. It was chaos.

I had a bath then wandered into my room. It looked a bit of a mess if I'm honest. The once hanging wallpaper had completely fallen off, revealing some very old, very dirty yellow patterns beneath it. It was incredibly unattractive and reminded me

of my father's ranch, of a time when I was poor and lonely and going nowhere. I always said I'd die before I became that person again.
When I got dressed, I went through to where the telephone stood and dialed Marshal again. The phone rang about four times before being cut off entirely. I was confused, but I figured he probably hadn't gotten to work yet.

Rain pounded the windows harder than ever. I knew I'd have to leave eventually. My wife was on the sofa catching rest for another empty day. It was as good a time as any to head out for work. Luckily a shiny cab was wadding through the street as I exited the doors and saw my signal to pull over. The driver had today's edition of the "New York Times" so I took off my rain jacket and flicked through it. I didn't make it further than the first page before the heading caused my heart to stop.

Wall Street's Darkest Hour

Share prices crumbled on stock exchanges around the world this morning as a financial panic sweeps the markets. The decline is of epic proportions. Furthermore, the stock exchange has faced a gut-wrenching collapse – far worse than those recorded from the financial panics that plagued the nation in decades gone by. The Dow Jones industrial average, the most widely watched measure of stock values on Wall Street, buckled by 309.32 points.

It closed in at 1223.41. The devastation has erased $50 Billion worth of stocks at this time, and the figure is only rising. The decline has been in the making for a long while, but stock companies, brokers, newspapers, and the government have glossed over issues to keep the public eye out of the loop. This is now to the detriment of millions of Americans who have entrusted their money into stocks, wall

street and other assets. The government claims it will go ahead with the world's largest shares sale ...

I'd read enough. I kept on hounding the driver to get me to work in a quicker time. I needed to ring my broker. To make sure my shares had been sold in time. To make sure it wasn't true. Then I'd feel better. My office was on the wrong side of Wall Street though. I had to pass through it and go a few blocks to get there. Just as we pulled onto Wall Street with the intent of driving through I could see there was a problem.
The street was lined with panic.
Doors were barred shut against angry men filled with fiery desperation. Many grey faces sat on the curb, absorbing the rain, hoping it would wash away their panic. There was a mixture of those in pain but still holding onto hope with those whose only hope was to drown quietly. I left the began to run. I felt a labyrinth of emotions as I ran past everyone. Rain gushed over every part of me, but I didn't spare

an ounce of care. I passed a man crying into a puddle, a man taking his anger out on a company sign, a limp body hurled from many floors above. The latter caught my eye the most. It made me run a little faster.
Finally, I reached the firm, it was eerily quiet inside. Like a safe house surrounded by a city on fire. I threw myself up the stairs three at a time. I slipped as I turned onto the final flight. My legged smashed into the railing, making a cracking sound on impact. But I didn't let myself feel it. I kept on running. I pushed open the doors and paced across the room until I spotted a telephone.

I dialed the number incorrectly three times. The fourth time I made sure it was correct. It didn't ring. I tried it again. Then again. Then again. It just didn't ring, I think the line had been cut off. I felt paralyzed and helpless, but I wasn't done yet. I bolted back down the stairs, through the hall and out of the building, heading in the direction my broker worked. I ran like a man who hadn't given up hope. From my memory, I knew it wasn't too far a distance from the firm but it felt like an eternity when your futures on the line.

Soon enough, the doors were in front of me. I barged through them to find the reception had become a haven of anger and fear as people were flooding in to find answers. I just headed straight for the stairs. I knew my broker worked on the fourth floor in room seven. I walked as quickly as my injured leg would allow until I reached his office. I knew it was the right room, his name plaque on the door told me so. I walked in to find a desolate room. It was a white box with a view onto an alleyway, but I wasn't interested in the aesthetics. It was pretty much empty. It had been abandoned. God knows where he went. I sunk onto the floor of the room, it was over, I had been played.

I sat for no less than three hours, I was just

thinking. I'm not sure if I had fully taken in what was happening, I was simply in a state of blankness. I knew the chaos ensuing outside was only worsening, yet all I could hear was myself, my own exhausted breathing. I felt betrayed, exhausted and empty as I laid there. I just didn't see a point in carrying on. All the paths life seemed to take me on were shrouded with failure. In the corner of my eye I spotted a telephone, it had been left in the corner and was unplugged. Suddenly, an idea filled my head. I rose up very slowly and walked towards the telephone, picked it up and dialed the number of Mark Devlin. All the while I was holding on to the hope he had been sent the money before the panic of this morning, I prayed for this to be the case. Mark picked up with relative haste, allowing me to cut straight to the point. "Mark, did you get the money this morning? Did he send it to you? Have you given it to them? Is it all going to be –" "John stop" He shouted. "I haven't gotten the money, John. I'm afraid to say it's probably gone or worth nothing. A very long pause entered the call line. "You won't have an advantage over the other candidates so you'll have to get it from your own merit. You will need to have been the best." I said nothing, I just sort of stood there in a state of paralysis. Then Mark continued, "Look old chap, I'm sorry this happened, but you've gotta realize this is business and in business –." I ended the call be throwing the telephone across the room. I pulled myself up and left the room. I walked through the chaos back to my apartment. People were packing up and leaving, jumping from buildings and breaking down on the street. The crowds outside the doors of banks and brokerages had swelled. The people had given up. Rain still hounded me, but I had grown used to it. I walked in just my shirt and trousers, I didn't see the point in putting back on my jacket and tie. I had made a decision on what I was going to do. A decision that would mean my tie and jacket would never be needed again.

I thought of my father, of the advice he gave me. Advice I tried so hard to fight and run away from that had caught up to me, pinned me down and drained everything from me. It turns out the world did have a way of dragging people back to where they came from. My mind then switched to my wife. She'd undoubtedly want to leave me. She probably wouldn't because it's not the done thing. But she'd want to. She'd have affairs and forget about me and wish me dead. I guess it's what I deserve because I filled her head with promises I couldn't keep.

Then I thought of my job, the one I'd never escape, or be promoted from or be happy in. I'd blown it. There was no point in it anymore. My leg was really hurting now, I was pretty much hobbling through the watery streets. Somehow the door to my apartment found me and I stumbled through. It was cold and empty, and I knew what I had to do.

It took me a long time to write the note. I wanted it to be perfect. I wanted something in my life to be perfect. Nothing was working though, I know my thought process was shot, but it was just so hard to make sense. Eventually, I just wrote what came to my head, plain and simple.

Dear ...

I'm lost without a cause at this point. I hope you read this.

Understand there was no other fate for me. I failed as a man, a lawyer, a son, and a husband. Forgive me. Remember me for my wit and charm and not my fallen grace.
I tried to make it in this world, but it's too tough a place. It's best for me to slip out quietly. I read once your true purpose is to be loved, and I guess I've lost my purpose.
I know now that people love a winner, so please don't have loved me.
I was once my own friend but now only

disgust and hate stare back in the mirror. There is something that this city has taught me … All good enemies begin as friends, I don't want to live in a world where this is the case anymore. Which means its time to go. Thank you for taking the time to think of me, even if it's only when I'm gone.

Goodbye.

I walked into my room and put on my best clothes. A maroon suit with matching braces, a silk bow tie and a black hat I wear for special occasions. My shoes were a little dirty so I gave them a polish, I was always taught well-polished shoes said a lot about a guy. I put the letter in my breast pocket and walked out to the balcony. Never looking back and not looking down I took the step. It was quick. It was painless. It was easy.

A short, bearded policeman walked into the apartment to find a grieving woman sat amongst a bed of tears on the floor. Her makeup ran off her face and her eyes were tired of producing tears. She looked up, trying to wipe the pain from her face, even in dark hours she needed to look presentable. “Mrs. Southland, a letter was found in your husband’s pocket. Though the erm… the blood has sort of made it unreadable in areas.” She took the letter and put it next to her pile of books and clothes. She spoke softly, “Is that all officer?”
“No well, there is this letter that was just delivered to the door, it was addressed to your husband. She took the letter from

him as he showed himself to the door. It was a small envelope with a golden crest on the front. Her long nails sliced through the paper, pulling out the letter out with a sense of guilt. This wasn't hers to open. She unfolded the paper and took a long few sec onds to read it. Her hand clasp ing her mouth as she did.

Dear Mr. John Southland,

On behalf of the Layton and Wilkins, we would like to invite you to the position of partner within our ...

Printed in Great Britain
by Amazon